PUFFIN BOOKS

DIARY OF A WIMPY KID

RODRICK RULES

OTHER BOOKS BY JEFF KINNEY

Diary of a Wimpy Kid

Coming soon:

Diary of a Wimpy Kid: The Last Straw

DIARY
of a
Wimpy Kid

RODRICK RULES

by Jeff Kinney

PUFFIN

PUFFIN BOOKS

Published by the Penguin Group
Penguin Books Ltd, 80 Strand, London WC2R ORL, England
Penguin Group (USA) Inc., 375 Hudson Street, New York, New York 10014, USA
Penguin Group (Canada), 90 Eglinton Avenue East, Suite 700, Toronto, Ontario, Canada M4P 2Y3
(a division of Pearson Penguin Canada Inc.)
Penguin Ireland, 25 St Stephen's Green, Dublin 2, Ireland (a division of Penguin Books Ltd)
Penguin Group (Australia), 250 Camberwell Road, Camberwell, Victoria 3124, Australia
(a division of Pearson Australia Group Pty Ltd)
Penguin Books India Pvt Ltd, 11 Community Centre, Panchsheel Park, New Delhi – 110 017, India
Penguin Group (NZ), 67 Apollo Drive, Rosedale, North Shore 0632, New Zealand
(a division of Pearson New Zealand Ltd)
Penguin Books (South Africa) (Pty) Ltd, 24 Sturdee Avenue, Rosebank,
Johannesburg 2196, South Africa

Penguin Books Ltd, Registered Offices: 80 Strand, London WC2R ORL, England

puffinbooks.com

First published in the English language in 2008 by Harry N. Abrams, Incorporated, New York
Original English title: *Rodrick Rules: Diary of a Wimpy Kid (book two)*
(All rights reserved in all countries by Harry N. Abrams, Inc.)
Published in Great Britain in Puffin Books 2009
This edition published 2014
008

Copyright © Jeff Kinney, 2008
Book design by Jeff Kinney
Cover design by Chad W. Beckerman and Jeff Kinney
All rights reserved

The moral right of the author/illustrator has been asserted

Made and printed in England by Clays Ltd, St Ives plc

British Library Cataloguing in Publication Data
A CIP catalogue record for this book is available from the British Library

ISBN: 978-0-141-35802-4

www.greenpenguin.co.uk

MIX
Paper from
responsible sources
FSC   FSC™ C018179
www.fsc.org

Penguin Books is committed to a sustainable
future for our business, our readers and our planet.
This book is made from Forest Stewardship
Council™ certified paper.

TO JULIE, WILL AND GRANT

SEPTEMBER

Monday

I guess Mom was pretty proud of herself for making me write in that journal last year, because now she went and bought me another one.

But remember how I said that if some jerk caught me carrying a book with "diary" on the cover, they were gonna get the wrong idea? Well, that's exactly what happened today.

(MY BROTHER RODRICK)

Now that Rodrick knows I have another journal, I better remember to keep this one locked up. Rodrick actually got hold of my LAST journal a few weeks back, and it was a disaster. But don't even get me started on THAT story.

Even without my Rodrick problems, my summer was pretty lousy.

Our family didn't go anywhere or do anything fun, and that's Dad's fault. Dad made me join the swim team again, and he wanted to make sure I didn't miss any meets this year.

Dad's got this idea that I'm destined to be a great swimmer or something, so that's why he makes me join the team every summer.

At my first swim meet a couple of years ago, Dad told me that when the umpire shot off the starter pistol, I was supposed to dive in and start swimming.

But what he DIDN'T tell me was that the starter gun only fired BLANKS.

So I was a whole lot more worried about where the bullet was gonna land than I was about getting myself to the other end of the pool.

Even after Dad explained the whole "starter pistol" concept to me, I was still the worst swimmer on the team.

But I did end up winning "Most Improved" at the awards banquet at the end of the summer. That's only because there was a ten-minute difference between my first race and my last one.

So I guess Dad's still waiting for me to live up to my potential.

In a lot of ways, being on the swim team was worse than being in middle school.

First of all, we had to be at the pool by 7:30 every morning, and the water was always FREEZING cold.

And, second of all, we were all crammed into two lanes, so I always had somebody on my tail trying to get round me.

The reason we had to use two lanes was because swim practice was at the same time as the Water Jazz class.

I actually tried to convince Dad to let me do Water Jazz instead of swim team, but he wouldn't go for it.

This was the first summer the coach let us boys wear swimming trunks instead of those skimpy racing trunks. But Mom said Rodrick's hand-me-down bathing suit was "perfectly fine".

After swim practice, Rodrick would pick me up in his band's van. Mom had this crazy idea that if me and Rodrick spent "quality time" on the ride home every day, we wouldn't fight as much. But all it did was make things a lot worse.

Rodrick was always a half hour late picking me up.

And he wouldn't let me sit up front. He said the chlorine would ruin his seat, even though the van is something like fifteen years old.

Rodrick's van doesn't actually have any seats in the back, so I had to squeeze in with all the band equipment. And every time the van came to a stop, I had to pray I didn't get my head taken off by one of Rodrick's drums.

I ended up walking home every day instead of getting a ride from Rodrick. I figured it was better to just walk the two miles than to get brain damage riding in the back of that van.

Halfway through the summer, I decided I was pretty much done with swim team. So I came up with a trick to get out of practice.

I'd swim a few laps, and then ask the coach if I could use the bathroom. Then I'd just hide out in the locker room until practice was over.

The only problem with my plan was that it was something like zero degrees in the boys' bathroom. So it was even colder in THERE than it was in the pool.

I had to wrap myself up in toilet paper so I didn't get hypothermia.

That's how I spent a pretty big chunk of my summer holidays. And that's why I'm actually looking forward to going back to school tomorrow.

Tuesday
When I got to school today, everybody was acting all strange around me, and at first I didn't know WHAT was up.

Then I remembered: I still had the Cheese Touch from LAST year. I got the Cheese Touch in the last week of school, and over the summer I COMPLETELY forgot about it.

The problem with the Cheese Touch is that you've got it until you can pass it on to someone else. But nobody would even get within thirty feet of me, so I knew I was gonna be stuck with the Cheese Touch for the whole school year.

Luckily, there was a new kid named Jeremy Pindle in homeroom, so that took care of THAT problem.

My first class was Pre-Algebra, and the teacher put me right next to Alex Aruda, the smartest kid in the whole class.

Alex is SUPER easy to copy from, because he always finishes his test early and puts his paper down on the floor next to him. So if I ever get in a pinch, it's nice to know I can count on Alex to bail me out.

Kids whose last names start with the first few letters of the alphabet get called on the most by the teacher, and that's why they end up being the smartest.

Some people think that's not true, but if you want to come down to my school, I can prove it.

ALEX ARUDA   CHRISTOPHER ZIEGEL

I can only think of ONE kid who broke the last-name rule, and that's Peter Uteger. Peter was the smartest kid in the class all the way up until the fifth grade.

That's when a bunch of us started giving him a hard time about how his initials sounded when you said them out loud.

These days, Peter doesn't raise his hand at ALL, and he's pretty much a C student.

I guess I feel a little bad about the whole P.U. thing and what happened to Peter. But it's hard not to take credit whenever it comes up.

Anyway, today I got pretty decent seats in all my classes except seventh-period History. My teacher is Mr Huff, and something tells me he had Rodrick as a student a few years back.

MR HEFFLEY, YOU'LL BE SITTING IN THIS CHAIR NEXT TO MY DESK.

Wednesday

Mom has been making me and Rodrick help out more around the house, and now the two of us are responsible for doing the dishes every night.

The rule is that we're not allowed to watch any TV or play video games until all the dishes are done. But let me just say that Rodrick is the WORST dishes partner in the world.

As soon as dinner is over, he goes upstairs to the bathroom and camps out there for an hour. And by the time he comes back downstairs, I'm already done.

But if I ever complain to Mom and Dad, Rodrick always pulls out the same lame excuse:

I think Mom and Dad are too worried about my little brother, Manny, to get involved in a fight between me and Rodrick right now anyway.

Yesterday, Manny drew a picture at nursery, and Mom and Dad got really upset when they found it in his backpack.

Mom and Dad thought the picture was supposed to be of THEM, so now they're acting all lovey in front of Manny.

I LOVE YOU SOOOO MUCH!

AND I LOVE YOU SO MUCH!

I knew who it was REALLY supposed to be in the picture: me and Rodrick.

We got into a big blowout over the remote control the other night, and Manny was there to witness the whole thing. But Mom and Dad don't need to find out about THAT.

Thursday
Another reason my summer was kind of lame was because my best friend, Rowley, was on holiday pretty much the whole time. I think he went to South America or something but, to be honest with you, I'm not really sure.

I don't know if this makes me a bad person or whatever, but it's hard for me to get interested in other people's holidays.

AND THEN WE'RE GONNA GET ON A BOAT AND CRUISE DOWN THIS RIVER...

MM HMM...HEY, HAVE YOU EVER NOTICED THIS FRECKLE BEFORE?

Besides, it seems like Rowley's family is always travelling to some crazy place in the world, and I can never keep their trips straight.

The other reason I don't care about Rowley's trips is because whenever Rowley comes back from one of his holidays, he always crams it down my throat.

Last year, Rowley and his family went to Australia for ten days, but from the way he acted when he got back you'd think he lived there his whole life.

Another thing that's really annoying is that whenever Rowley goes to some new country, he gets into whatever fad is going on over there.

Like when Rowley got back from Europe two years ago, he got hooked on this pop singer named "Joshie", who I guess is some huge star or something. So Rowley came back with his bags full of Joshie CDs and posters and stuff.

I took one look at the picture on the CD and told Rowley that Joshie was supposed to be for six-year-old girls, but he didn't believe me. Rowley said I was just jealous because he was the one who "discovered" Joshie.

And what made it really irritating was that now this guy was Rowley's new hero. So if I ever tried to say anything critical at all, Rowley didn't want to hear it.

Speaking of foreign countries, today in French class, Madame Lefrere told us we're going to be choosing pen pals this year.

When Rodrick was in middle school, he had a seventeen-year-old girl from Holland as his pen pal. I know because I've seen the letters in his junk drawer.

I like the
sunshiny
days &
ice cream.
Do you, too?
♡

When Madame Lefrere handed out the forms, I made sure I checked off the boxes that would get me a pen pal just like Rodrick's.

But after Madame Lefrere read over my form, she made me start over and pick again. She said I had to choose a boy who is my age, AND he has to be French. So I don't exactly have high hopes for my pen-pal experience.

Je m'appelle "Philippe".

Friday
Mom decided to start making Rodrick pick me up after school, just like he picked me up after swimming practice. I guess that means she didn't learn from THAT experience. But I did. So when Rodrick picked me up today, I asked him to please take it easy on the brakes.

Rodrick said OK, but then he went out of his way to find every speed bump in town.

When I got out of the van, I called Rodrick a big jerk, and then it got physical. Mom saw the whole thing unfold from the living-room window.

Mom made us come inside, and she sat us down at the kitchen table. Then she said me and Rodrick were going to have to settle our differences in a "civil manner".

Mom told me and Rodrick we each had to write down what we did wrong, and then we had to draw a picture to go along with it. And I knew exactly where Mom was going with THAT idea.

Mom used to be a pre-school teacher and, whenever a kid would do something wrong, she'd make him draw a picture of it. I guess the idea was to make the kid feel ashamed of what he did so he wouldn't do it again.

I will not break the crayons because that makes the other children very sad.

Well, Mom's idea might have worked great on a bunch of four-year-olds, but she's going to have to think of something better if she wants me and Rodrick to get along.

I will not call Rodrick names.

BUNNY RABBIT!

WAAAAH!

I will not push Gregory.

AIEEE!

The truth is, Rodrick can pretty much treat me any way he wants, because he knows there's nothing I can do about it.

See, Rodrick is the only one who knows about this REALLY embarrassing thing that happened to me over the summer, and he's been holding it over my head ever since. So if I ever tell on him for anything, he'll spill my secret to the whole world.

I just wish I had some dirt on HIM to even things out.

I do know ONE embarrassing thing about Rodrick, but I don't think it's gonna do me any good.

When Rodrick was a sophomore, he was sick the day they did school photos. So Mom told Dad to mail in Rodrick's freshman picture for the school to use in the yearbook.

Don't ask me how Dad screwed this up, but he sent in Rodrick's SECOND-grade picture.

And, believe it or not, it actually got printed.

| *Harrington,* | *Hatley,* | *Heffley,* | *Hills,* |
| *Leonard* | *Andrew* | *Rodrick* | *Heather* |

Unfortunately, Rodrick was smart enough to rip that page out of his yearbook. So if I'm ever gonna find something to use against him, I guess I have to keep digging.

Wednesday

Ever since Mom assigned the dishes to me and Rodrick, Dad's been going down to the furnace room after dinner to work on this miniature Civil War battlefield of his.

Dad spends at least three hours a night down there working on that thing. I think Dad would be happy to spend the whole weekend working on his battlefield, but Mom has OTHER plans for him.

Mom likes to rent these romantic comedies, and she makes Dad watch them with her. But I know Dad is just waiting for the first chance to break away and go back down to the basement.

Whenever Dad can't be down in the furnace room, he makes sure us kids keep away from it.

Dad won't let me or Rodrick go NEAR his battlefield, because he thinks we're gonna mess something up.

And earlier today I overheard Dad say something to Manny to make sure HE doesn't go poking around back there, either.

I THINK I JUST HEARD SOME GRUNTING NOISES COMING FROM THE FURNACE ROOM.

Saturday
Rowley came over to my house today. Dad doesn't like it when Rowley comes over, because Dad always says Rowley is "accident prone". I think it's because this one time Rowley was eating dinner here, and he dropped a plate and broke it.

So now Dad has this idea that Rowley is going to ruin his whole Civil War battlefield in one klutzy move.

Whenever Rowley comes over to my house these days, he gets the same greeting:

Rowley's dad doesn't like ME, either. That's why I don't go over to his house much any more.

The last time I spent the night at Rowley's, we watched this movie where some kids taught themselves a secret language that no grown-ups could understand.

TRANSLATION: AT EXACTLY 2:30 P.M., LET'S ALL DROP OUR BOOKS ON THE FLOOR.

Me and Rowley thought that was pretty cool, and we tried to figure out how to talk in the same language the kids were using in the movie.

But we couldn't really get the hang of it, so we made up our OWN secret language.

Then we tried it out at dinner.

But Rowley's dad must have cracked our code, because I ended up getting sent home before dessert. And I haven't been invited to spend the night at Rowley's ever since.

When Rowley came over to my house today, he
brought a bunch of pictures from his trip with
him. He said the best part of his holiday was
when they went on a river safari, and he showed
me all these blurry pictures of birds and stuff.

Now, I've been to the Wild Kingdom amusement
park a bunch of times, and they have this River
Rapids ride where they have these awesome robot
animals like gorillas and dinosaurs.

If you ask me, Rowley's parents should have just
saved their money and taken him there instead.

But of course Rowley didn't want to hear about MY experiences, so he just gathered up his pictures and went back home.

Tonight after dinner, Mom made Dad watch one of the movies she'd rented, but Dad really wanted to work on his Civil War battlefield.

When Mom got up to go to the bathroom, Dad stuffed a bunch of pillows under the blanket on his side of the bed to make it look like he was asleep.

Mom didn't find out about Dad's decoy until after the movie was over.

She made Dad come to bed, even though it was only 8:30.

And now Manny sleeps in Mom and Dad's bed, because he's afraid of the monster that lives in the furnace room.

Tuesday

I thought I was done hearing about Rowley's trip, but I was wrong. Yesterday, our Social Studies teacher asked Rowley to tell the class all about his holiday, and today he came to school wearing this ridiculous costume. But what was even WORSE was when some girls came up to Rowley at lunch and started kissing his butt.

But then I realized maybe that wasn't such a bad thing after all. So I started parading Rowley around the cafeteria, because, after all, he IS my best friend.

Saturday

Dad has been taking me to the mall every Saturday for the past few weeks. At first, I thought it was because he wanted to spend more time with me. But then I realized he's just making sure he's out of the house for Rodrick's band practices, which I can totally understand.

Rodrick and his heavy-metal band practise in the basement on weekends.

The lead singer of the band is this guy named Bill Walter, and me and Dad bumped into Bill on the way out the door today.

Bill doesn't have a job, and he still lives with his parents, even though he's thirty-five years old.

I'm pretty sure Dad's worst fear is that Rodrick is going to see Bill as some kind of role model, and that Rodrick will want to follow in Bill's footsteps.

So whenever Dad sees Bill, it just puts him in a bad mood for the rest of the day.

The reason Rodrick invited Bill to be in his band was because Bill got voted "Most Likely to Be a Rock Star" when HE was in high school.

Most Likely to Be a Rock Star

Bill Walter   Anna Wrentham

That hasn't really worked out for Bill yet. And I think I heard Anna Wrentham is in prison.

Anyway, me and Dad went to the mall for a few hours today, but when we got back, Rodrick's band practice wasn't over yet. You could hear the guitars and drums from a block away, and there was a bunch of random teenagers hanging out in our driveway.

I guess they must have heard the music coming out of the basement and got drawn to it, sort of like how moths get drawn to a light.

When Dad saw all those teenagers in the driveway, he TOTALLY freaked out.

Dad ran inside to call the cops, but Mom stopped him before he could dial 911.

Mom said those teenagers weren't doing any harm, and that they were just "appreciating" Rodrick's music. But I don't even know how she could say that with a straight face. And if you ever heard Rodrick's band, you'd know what I mean.

Dad couldn't relax with all those teenagers out in our driveway.

So he went upstairs and got his boom box. Then he put in a classical music CD and let it play. And you would not BELIEVE how quickly the driveway cleared out after that.

Dad was pretty proud of himself for thinking up that one. But Mom accused him of getting rid of Rodrick's "fans" on purpose.

Sunday

Today, on the car ride to church, I was making faces at Manny, trying to get him to laugh. I made this one face that made Manny laugh so hard that apple juice came out of his nose.

But then Mom said:

Well, once Mom put that thought in Manny's head, it was all over.

See? This is the reason I keep my distance from Manny. Every time I try to have a little fun with him, I end up regretting it.

I remember when I was younger, and Mom and Dad told me I was getting a little brother. I was REALLY excited.

After all those years of getting pushed around by Rodrick, I was definitely ready to move up a notch on the totem pole.

But Mom and Dad have always been SUPER protective of Manny, and they won't let me lay a finger on him, even if he totally deserves it.

Like the other day, I plugged in my video game system, and it wouldn't start. I opened it up and found out that Manny had stuffed a chocolate-chip cookie in the disc drive.

And of course Manny used the same excuse he ALWAYS uses when he breaks my stuff.

I really wanted to let Manny have it, but I couldn't do anything with Mom standing right there.

Mom said she would have a "talk" with Manny, and they went downstairs. A half hour later, they came back up to my room, and Manny was holding something in his hands.

It was a ball of tinfoil with a bunch of toothpicks sticking out of it.

Don't ask me how that was supposed to make up for my broken video game system. I went to throw the stupid thing away, but Mom wouldn't even let me do THAT.

YOUR BROTHER **MADE** THAT FOR YOU!

The first chance I get, that thing's going in the trash. Because, mark my words, if I don't get rid of it, I'm gonna end up sitting on it.

Even though Manny drives me totally nuts, there is ONE reason I like having him around. Ever since Manny started talking, Rodrick has stopped making me sell chocolate bars for his school fund-raisers. And, believe me, I'm grateful for THAT.

BEFORE...

UM...HELLO, SIR...WOULD YOU LIKE TO HELP SUPPORT...

NOT INTERESTED!

NOW...

WOOD YOU WIKE SOME CHOKWITS?

HOW PRECIOUS!

Monday

Madame Lefrere made us write our first pen-pal letters today. I got assigned to this kid named Mamadou Montpierre, and I guess he lives someplace in France.

I know I'm supposed to write in French and Mamadou is supposed to write in English, but, to be honest with you, writing in a foreign language is pretty hard.

So I really don't see the need for both of us to stress out over this whole pen-pal thing.

Dear Mamadou,

First of all, I think we should both just write in English to keep things simple.

By the way, remember how I said I was gonna end up sitting on Manny's spiky tinfoil ball thing? Well, I was half right.

45

Rowley came over today to play video games, and HE ended up sitting on it.

I'm actually kind of relieved, to be honest with you. I lost track of that thing a couple of days ago, and I'm just glad it finally turned up.

And in all the commotion, I threw Manny's "gift" in the garbage. But something tells me Mom wouldn't have stopped me this time.

Wednesday
Rodrick has an English paper due tomorrow, and Mom's actually making him do it himself for once. Rodrick doesn't know how to type, so he usually writes his papers out on notebook paper and then hands them off to Dad.

46

But when Dad reads over Rodrick's work, he finds all sorts of factual errors.

WELL, FOR STARTERS, ABRAHAM LINCOLN DIDN'T WRITE "TO KILL A MOCKINGBIRD".

Rodrick doesn't really care about the mistakes, so he tells Dad to just go ahead and type the paper like it is.

But Dad can't stand typing a paper with errors in it, so he just rewrites Rodrick's paper from scratch. And then a couple of days later, Rodrick brings his graded paper home and acts like he did it himself.

This has been going on for a few years, and I guess Mom decided she's going to put an end to it. So tonight she told Dad that Rodrick was going to have to do his OWN work this time round, and that Dad wasn't allowed to help out.

Rodrick went in the computer room after dinner, and you could hear him typing about one letter a minute.

I could tell the sound of Rodrick typing was driving Dad totally bananas. On top of that, Rodrick would come out of the computer room every ten minutes and ask Dad some dumb question.

WHERE'S THE SPACE BAR AGAIN?

After a couple of hours, Dad finally cracked.

Dad waited for Mom to go to bed, and then he typed Rodrick's whole paper for him. So I guess this means Rodrick's system is safe, at least for now.

I have a book report due tomorrow, but I'm really not sweating it.

I found the secret to doing book reports a long time ago. I've been milking the same book for the past five years: "Sherlock Sammy Does It Again".

There are about twenty short stories in
"Sherlock Sammy Does It Again", but I just
treat each story like it's a whole book, and the
teacher never notices.

These Sherlock Sammy stories are all the same.
Some grown-up commits a crime, and then
Sherlock Sammy figures it out and makes the
person look stupid.

YOUR FIRST MISTAKE, MR BEASLEY, WAS WHEN YOU FORGOT TO CONVERT CELSIUS TO FAHRENHEIT!

GEEK!

I'm kind of an expert at writing book reports
by now. All you have to do is write exactly what
the teacher wants to hear, and you're all set.

Man, Sherlock Sammy is so smart, and I'll bet that's cause he reads so many books.

I'll bet you're right!

There were a bunch of hard words in this book, but I looked them up in the dictionary so now I know what they mean.

I guess you're a bit of a "sleuth" yourself! (A+)

<u>Monday</u>

There was a kid named Chirag Gupta who was one of my friends last year, but he moved away in June. His family had a big going-away party, and the whole neighbourhood came. But I guess Chirag's family must have changed their mind, because today Chirag was back in school.

Everyone was happy to see Chirag again, but a couple of us decided to have a little fun with him before officially welcoming him back.

So we basically pretended he was still gone.

I have to admit, it was pretty funny.

At lunch, Chirag sat next to me. I had an
extra chocolate-chip cookie in my lunch bag, and
I made a big deal about it.

OK, so maybe that one was a little cruel.

(GOBBLE GOBBLE
SMACK SMACK)

I guess we'll probably let Chirag off the hook tomorrow. But, then again, this Invisible Chirag thing could turn into the next "P.U.".

Tuesday
OK, so the Invisible Chirag joke is still going, and the whole CLASS is in on it now. I don't want to get too far ahead of myself or anything, but I think I might have Class Clown in the bag for dreaming this one up.

In Science, the teacher asked me to count the number of kids in the classroom so she'd know how many pairs of safety goggles to get out of the closet.

So I made a big show of counting everyone in the room except Chirag.

...33...34!
THERE ARE 34
PEOPLE IN
THIS CLASS.

Well, that REALLY set Chirag off. He got up and started yelling, and it was really hard to stare straight ahead and act like he wasn't there.

I...AM...A...
HUMAN...
BEING...TOO!

55

I wanted to tell him that we never said he wasn't a human being, it's just that he's an INVISIBLE human being. But I managed to keep my mouth shut.

Before you go and say I'm a bad friend for teasing Chirag, let me just say this in my own defence: I'm smaller than about 95% of the kids at my school so, when it comes to finding someone I can actually pick on, my options are pretty limited.

And, besides, I'm not 100% to blame for dreaming up this idea. Believe it or not, I got the idea from Mom. This one time when I was a kid, I was playing under the kitchen table, and Mom came looking for me.

HAS ANYONE SEEN GREGORY?

I don't know what made me do it, but I decided to play a joke on Mom and stay hidden.

Mom went all around the house calling my name. I think she must have finally seen me under the kitchen table, but she still pretended she didn't know where I was.

POOR GREGORY, ALL ALONE IN THE SNOW. OH, BOO HOO HOO.

I thought it was pretty funny, and I probably would've stayed hidden under there for a little while more. But Mom finally got me to crack when she said she was gonna give my gum-ball machine to Rodrick.

So if you want to point fingers on the Invisible Chirag joke, now you know who's really to blame.

Thursday

Well, yesterday, Chirag pretty much gave up on trying to get anyone in our class to talk to him. But today he found our weakness.

I forgot ALL about Rowley. When the joke first started up, I made sure to keep him away from Chirag, because I had a feeling Rowley would blow the joke.

But I guess I kind of got too cocky and let my guard down.

Chirag started working on Rowley at lunch, and he came really close to getting him to crack.

IF YOU SAY I EXIST, THIS CORN DOG IS YOURS!

I could tell Rowley was about to say something, so I had to act quick. I told everyone there was a floating corn dog hovering above our lunch table, and then I plucked it out of the air and ate it in two bites.

So thanks to my quick thinking, we were able to keep the joke going.

But that REALLY made Chirag mad. He started punching my arm, but of course I had to pretend like I didn't notice.

And, let me tell you, that wasn't easy to do. Chirag might be small, but that kid can really punch.

<u>Friday</u>

Well, I guess Chirag must have complained to a teacher about my little joke, because today I got called down to the front office.

When I got to Vice Principal Roy's room, he was pretty mad. He knew all about how I started the joke, and he gave me a speech about "respect" and "decency" and all that.

But luckily Mr Roy got one crucial fact wrong, and that was the identity of the person we were playing the joke on. So that made the apology part a whole lot easier.

I AM DEEPLY SORRY, AND NOW I DO INDEED ADMIT THAT YOU EXIST, SHARIF.

Mr Roy seemed pretty satisfied with my apology and he let me go without even tacking on any detention.

I've always heard that when Mr Roy is done chewing a kid out, he sends them off with a pat on the back and a lollipop. And now I can tell you firsthand that it's true.

Saturday
Rowley's birthday party is tomorrow, so Mom took me to the mall to get him a gift. I picked out this cool video game that just came out, and I handed it to Mom so she could pay for it. But Mom said I had to buy it with my OWN money.

I told Mom that, first of all, I have zero money.

And, second of all, if I DID have any money, I wouldn't be wasting it on ROWLEY.

Mom didn't seem too happy with what I said, but it's not MY fault I'm broke. I actually had a job this summer, but the people I worked for stiffed me, so I didn't earn a single penny.

We have these neighbours named the Fullers who live a few doors up, and they go away on holiday every summer.

They usually leave their dog, Princess, in the kennel, but this year, they told me they'd pay me five bucks a day to feed Princess and take her out. I figured out I'd earn enough to buy a whole pile of video games with that kind of money.

But I guess Princess is gun-shy about going to the bathroom in front of strangers, so I ended up spending a lot of time standing around in the hot sun waiting for this dumb dog to hurry up and go.

I'd wait and wait and nothing would happen, and then I'd just take Princess back inside.

But EVERY time I'd leave, Princess would make a big mess in the foyer, and I'd have to clean it up the next day. Towards the end of the summer I got smart and realized it would be a whole lot easier to just clean up all of Princess's messes at once instead of doing it every single day.

So I fed her and let her do her business on the foyer floor for about two weeks.

Then, the day before the Fullers were due back, I headed up the hill with all my cleaning supplies.

But guess what? The Fullers cut their trip short and got home a day EARLY.

I guess they didn't know it's polite to call ahead and let people know when your plans have changed.

Tonight, Mom called a house meeting with me and Rodrick. She said that the two of us are always complaining that we don't have any money, so she came up with a way for us to earn some cash.

Then she pulled out some play money she must've dug up out of a board game, and she called the money "Mom Bucks". Mom said we could earn Mom Bucks by doing chores and good deeds and stuff like that, and we could trade them in for REAL money.

Mom handed us $1,000 each to get us started. I thought I had struck it rich. But then she explained that each Mom Buck was only worth a penny of REAL money.

Mom told us how we should save up our Mom Bucks and, if we were patient, we could buy something we really wanted.

But Rodrick cashed in his whole stash before Mom
was even done talking.

Then he went down to the convenience store and
blew his money on some heavy-metal magazines.

If Rodrick wants to waste his money like that,
he can go right ahead. But I'm gonna be smart
with MY Mom Bucks.

Sunday
Today was Rowley's birthday party, and he had it
at the mall. I'm sure I would have thought it was
a lot of fun if I was about seven years old.

That was the average age of the kids at Rowley's party. Rowley invited his whole karate team, and most of those kids are still in elementary school. I just wish I could have known what the party was gonna be like so I could have skipped it.

We started off playing these dopey party games like Pin the Tail on the Donkey and stuff like that. The last game we played was Hide-and-Seek.

My plan was to just hide in the ball pit and stay there until the party was over. But some OTHER kid was already in there.

It turned out this kid wasn't from Rowley's party. He was from the LAST birthday party that happened an hour earlier.

I guess he must have hidden in there during Hide-and-Seek, and nobody ever FOUND him.

So Rowley's party had to be put on hold while the staff tried to track down this kid's parents.

After that situation got cleared up, we had cake and watched Rowley open his gifts. He mostly got a bunch of kids' toys, but he seemed pretty happy about it.

Then Rowley's parents gave him their present. And guess what? It was a DIARY.

It kind of ticked me off, because I knew Rowley asked his parents for a diary so he could be just like me. After Rowley opened his present he said:

I let him know exactly what I thought of that idea by slugging him in the arm. And I really don't care that it was his birthday, either.

One thing I will say, though. I used to be mad at Mom for getting me a journal that looked too girly. But, after seeing Rowley's diary, I'm not so mad any more.

Lately, Rowley has been TOTALLY bugging me. He reads the same comic books I read, drinks the same kind of soda I drink, you name it. Mom says I should be "flattered", but to be honest with you, it's totally creeping me out.

A couple of days ago, I did an experiment to see just how far Rowley would go.

I rolled up one of my trouser legs and tied a
bandanna round my ankle and went to school
that way.

Sure enough, the next day Rowley came to school
wearing the same exact thing.

And that's how I ended up in Vice Principal
Roy's office for the second time in a week.

THERE ARE SOME
THUGS OUTSIDE MY
HOUSE SPORTING
"GANG COLOURS".

Monday
I thought I was totally in the clear for the
Invisible Chirag thing. But, boy, was I wrong.

Tonight, Mom got a call from Chirag's DAD. Mr Gupta told Mom all about the prank we were playing on his son, and how I was the ringleader.

When Mom questioned me, I told her I didn't even know what Chirag's dad was talking about.

Then Mom marched me up to Rowley's house to hear what HE had to say.

Luckily, I was prepared for this kind of thing. I had already drilled Rowley on what to do if we ever got busted, and that if we both just denied everything we'd be OK.

But the second Mom started asking Rowley questions, he broke down.

So after our visit to Rowley's house, Mom drove me over to Chirag's to apologize. And, let me tell you, THAT wasn't a whole lot of fun.

Mr Gupta didn't seem too impressed with my apology, but, believe it or not, Chirag was actually pretty cool about it.

After I apologized, Chirag invited me inside to play video games. I think he was so relieved to finally have one of his classmates talking to him again that he just decided to forgive me for the whole incident.

So I guess I forgive him, too.

Tuesday
Even though Chirag let me off the hook last night, Mom wasn't done with me yet.

She wasn't really that mad about the joke or how I treated Chirag. She was just mad that I LIED about it.

So Mom told me she'll ground me for a MONTH if she catches me lying again.

And that means I better watch my step, because Mom's not gonna forget what she said. When it comes to my screw-ups, Mom has a memory like an elephant.

THAT'S THE SECOND TIME YOU TRACKED MUD INTO THE KITCHEN!

(FIRST TIME: SIX YEARS AGO)

Last year Mom caught me lying, and I paid the price for it.

Mom made a gingerbread house a week before Christmas, and she put it on top of the refrigerator. She said nobody was allowed to touch it until Christmas Eve dinner.

But I couldn't help myself. So every night, I'd sneak downstairs and pick off a little piece of the gingerbread house. I tried to only eat a tiny piece each time so Mom wouldn't notice.

It was really hard to limit myself to one gumdrop or one little crumb of gingerbread each night, but I managed to do it anyway.

I didn't know how much I had actually eaten until Mom took it down off the fridge on Christmas Eve.

When Mom accused me of eating all the candy, I denied it. But I wish I'd just fessed up right away, because that fib totally backfired on me.

Mom had just been hired to write a parenting column for the local newspaper, and she was always looking for material. So that incident pretty much made me into a local celebrity.

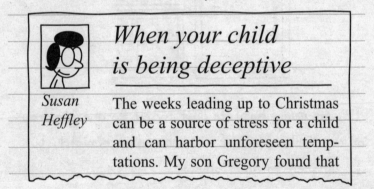

When your child is being deceptive

Susan Heffley

The weeks leading up to Christmas can be a source of stress for a child and can harbor unforeseen temptations. My son Gregory found that

You know, now that I think about it, Mom isn't exactly squeaky clean when it comes to being honest HERSELF.

I remember when I was a kid, and she found out I wasn't brushing my teeth every night. She faked a call to the dentist's office. And that call is the reason why I still brush my teeth four times a day.

DR KRATZ, DO YOU HAVE DENTURES FOR LITTLE BOYS? OH, ONLY WOODEN ONES? I GUESS THAT WILL HAVE TO DO, THEN.

Friday
Well, it's been three days and I've kept my promise to Mom. I've been 100% honest the whole time, and, believe it or not, it's not that hard.

In fact, it's kind of liberating. I've been in a couple of situations already where I was a lot more honest than I would have been a week ago.

For example, the other day I had a conversation with this neighbourhood kid named Shawn Snella.

And, yesterday, Rowley's family had a birthday party for his grandfather.

Most people don't seem to appreciate a person as honest as me. So don't ask me how George Washington ever got to be president.

<u>Saturday</u>

Today I answered the phone, and it was Mrs Gillman from the PTA, looking for Mom. I tried to hand her the phone, but she whispered for me to tell Mrs Gillman that she wasn't home.

I couldn't tell if Mom was trying to trick me into lying or WHAT, but there was no way I was going to break my honesty streak over something as dumb as THIS.

So I made Mom go out on the front porch before I said a word to Mrs Gillman.

MY MOTHER IS NOT INSIDE THE HOUSE RIGHT NOW.

And from the look Mom gave me when she came back in the house, I kind of get the feeling she's not gonna hold me to that honesty pledge any more.

Monday
Today was Career Day at school. They have Career Day every year to get us kids to start thinking about our future.

They brought in a bunch of adults who had all these different jobs. I think the idea is that us kids will find out about a job we like, and then we'll know what we want to be when we grow up.

But what REALLY happens is that you just find out which jobs to rule out.

After the presentations, we had to fill out these questionnaires. The first question was, "Where do you see yourself in fifteen years?"

I know EXACTLY where I'll be in fifteen years: in my pool, at my mansion, counting my money. But there weren't any check boxes for THAT option.

The questionnaires are supposed to predict what kind of job you're going to have when you grow up. When I was finished, I looked up my job on the chart, and I got "Clerk".

Well, there must be something wrong with the way they set these forms up or something, because I don't know any clerks who are billionaires.

Some other kids were unhappy with the jobs they ended up with, too. But the teacher said we shouldn't take these things too seriously.

Well, try telling that to Edward Mealey. Last year, he got "Sanitation Worker" on his job chart, and the teachers have been treating him differently ever since.

Rowley got "Nurse" on his job chart, and he seemed pretty happy about it. A couple of girls got Nurse, too, and they were chatting away with Rowley after class.

Next year I have to remember to sit next to
Rowley and copy his job form so I can get in on
some of that action.

Saturday
Me and Rodrick were just sitting around the
house today, so Mom sent us over to Gramma's to
rake her leaves.

Mom said she'd pay us $100 in Mom Bucks for
each bag we filled. Plus, Gramma said she'd give us
hot chocolate after we were finished.

I really didn't feel like working on a Saturday,
but I needed the cash. Besides, Gramma makes
really awesome hot chocolate. So we got some
rakes and plastic bags from our garage and
headed down to Gramma's house.

I took one side of the yard, and Rodrick took the other. But, ten minutes into the job, Rodrick came over and told me I was doing everything all wrong.

Rodrick said I was putting WAY too many leaves in each bag, and that if I just tied the bag closer to the bottom, I could get done a lot quicker.

See, now this is the kind of advice you're SUPPOSED to get from your older brother.

After Rodrick showed me that trick, we went through bags like nobody's business. In fact, we ran out in half an hour.

Gramma didn't seem too happy about forking over the hot chocolate when we came inside. But, like they say, a deal's a deal.

Monday
Ever since Career Day, Rowley has been spending lunch with a bunch of girls who sit at the corner table in the cafeteria. I guess the group of them is like the Future Nurses of America or something.

Don't ask me WHAT they talk about over there.
They just whisper and giggle like a bunch of
first-graders.

All I can say is, they better not be talking
about ME.

You remember how I said Rodrick is the only one
who knows about that really embarrassing thing
that happened to me over the summer? Well,
Rowley knows the SECOND most embarrassing
thing that ever happened to me, and I really
don't need him digging it back up.

Back in fifth grade, we had a project in Spanish
where we had to do a skit in front of the class,
and my partner was Rowley.

We had to do the whole skit in Spanish. Rowley asked me what I would do for a candy bar, and I said I'd stand on my head.

But when I tried to do a headstand, I tipped over, and my rear end went right through the wall.

ESTARIO
PARADO
EN MI
AY-AY-AY!

Well, the school never bothered to fix the hole, so for the rest of my time in elementary school, my butt-print was on display in Mrs Gonzales's room.

And if Rowley's spreading that story around, believe me I'm gonna tell the whole world who ate the Cheese.

<u>Wednesday</u>

Today I realized that if I wanted to know what Rowley and those girls are talking about at lunch, all I have to do is read his DIARY. I'll bet he's writing down all sorts of juicy gossip in that thing.

The problem is, Rowley's diary is LOCKED. So even if I got hold of it, I wouldn't have any way to open it. But then I thought of something. All I had to do was buy the same exact diary HE has, and then I'd have a key.

So I went to the bookstore tonight and got the last one on the shelf. I just hope buying this thing was worth it, because I had to cash in half of my Mom Bucks to pay for it. And I don't think Dad was too thrilled with the idea of me buying a Sweet Secrets Diary, either.

<u>Thursday</u>
After Phys Ed today, I saw that Rowley accidentally left his diary on the bench. So when the coast was clear, I used my new key on his diary and, sure enough, it worked.

I opened it up and started reading.

Dear Diary,
    Today I played with my Dinoblazer action figures again. It was Mecharex vs Triceraclops and Mecharex bited Triceraclops in the tail.

OW! DARN.

> And then Triceraclops
> turned round and
> said oh yeah well how
> do you like _that_ and
> he shot Mecharex right
> in the heinie.
>
> OW NO FAIR.

I flipped through the rest of the book to see if my name was in there anywhere, but it was just page after page of this garbage.

After seeing what's going on in Rowley's head, I'm kind of starting to wonder why I'm even friends with him in the first place.

Saturday

Things at home have been really good for about a week. Rodrick has the flu, so he doesn't have the energy to bother me. And Manny has been at Gramma's, so I've had the TV all to myself.

Yesterday, Mom and Dad made a surprise announcement. They said they were going away for the night, and that me and Rodrick were in charge of the house.

That was some pretty big news, because Mom and Dad have NEVER left me and Rodrick on our own before.

I think they've always been afraid that if they go away, Rodrick is gonna have a huge party and trash the house.

But with Rodrick knocked out with the flu, they must've seen their big chance. So after Mom gave us a speech about "responsibility" and "trust" and all that, they took off.

The SECOND Mom and Dad walked out of the door, Rodrick jumped up off of the couch and picked up the phone. Then he called every friend he knew and told them he was having a party.

I thought about calling Mom and Dad to tell them what Rodrick was up to, but I've never actually BEEN to a high-school party before, so I was curious. I decided to just keep my mouth shut and soak it all in.

Rodrick told me to get some folding tables out of the basement and bring a couple of bags of ice out of the downstairs freezer. Rodrick's friends started to show up around 7:00 and, before you knew it, there were cars parked up and down the street.

95

The first person to walk through the door was
Rodrick's friend Ward. A bunch more people
started showing up after that, and Rodrick told
me we were gonna need more tables. So I went
downstairs to get them.

But, as soon as I stepped foot in the basement,
I heard the door lock behind me.

I pounded on the door, but Rodrick just
cranked up the music to drown me out. So I was
stuck down there.

Man, I should've known Rodrick would go and
pull something like that.

I guess it was pretty dumb of me to think Rodrick was gonna let me in on the action.

It sounded like it was a pretty wild party. I think some GIRLS even showed up at one point, but I couldn't be too sure, because it was hard to keep track of what was going on from just looking at the bottoms of people's shoes.

The party was still going strong at 2:00 a.m., but that's when I gave up. I spent the night on one of the spare beds in the basement, even though there were no blankets on it. I practically froze to death, but there was no WAY I was gonna use a blanket from Rodrick's bed.

Somebody must've unlocked the basement door overnight, because when I woke up this morning, it was open. And when I walked upstairs, it looked like a tornado had touched down in the family room.

The last of Rodrick's friends wasn't gone until 3:00 in the afternoon. And, once everyone left, Rodrick told me I had to help him clean up.

I told Rodrick he was out of his mind if he thought I was helping. But then Rodrick said that if he got busted for the party, he was taking ME down with him.

He said if I didn't help him clean up the mess, he would tell all my friends about the thing that happened to me this summer.

I couldn't believe Rodrick would play dirty like that. But I could tell he was serious, so I just got to work.

VROOM

Mom and Dad were supposed to be back by 7:00, and we still had a TON of work to do.

It wasn't easy to erase all the evidence of the party, because Rodrick's friends had left trash in all these crazy places. At one point, when I went to make myself a bowl of cereal, a half-eaten piece of pizza fell out of the box.

By 6:45, we had things pretty well wrapped up. I went upstairs to take a shower, and that's when I saw the message written on the inside of the bathroom door.

I tried scrubbing the writing off with soap and water, but whoever wrote that thing must've used a permanent marker.

Mom and Dad were gonna be home any minute, so I thought we were doomed. But then Rodrick had a genius idea. He said we could switch the door and REPLACE it with a closet door from the basement.

So we got some screwdrivers and went to work.

We finally managed to get the door off its
hinges, and then we carried it downstairs.

Then we got the closet door from Rodrick's room
in the basement and brought it UPSTAIRS.

We made it with no time to spare. Mom and Dad's car rolled into the driveway right when we were tightening the last screw.

You could tell they were pretty relieved the house hadn't burned down while they were away.

I don't think we're totally out of the woods just yet. Because, with the way Dad was poking around tonight, I'm sure it won't be long before he figures out about the party.

Well, Rodrick might have lucked out this time, but all I can say is, he should be glad MANNY wasn't there to see the party. Manny is a HUGE tattletale. In fact, he's been telling on me ever since he could talk. He's even told on me for stuff I did BEFORE he could talk.

When I was a kid, I broke the sliding glass door in the family room. Mom and Dad didn't have any evidence that I was the one who did it, so they couldn't peg it on me, and I was in the clear. But Manny was there when it happened, and two years later, he squealed on me.

So after Manny started talking, I had to worry about all the bad things he saw me do when he was a baby.

I used to be a big tattletale myself until I learned my lesson. One time, I told on Rodrick for saying a bad word. Mom asked me which word he said, so I spelled it out. And it was a long one, too.

Well, I ended up getting a bar of soap in my mouth for knowing how to spell a bad word, and Rodrick got off scot-free.

Monday

Tomorrow, I have an English assignment due where I have to write an "allegory".

That's basically a story that says one thing but means something else. I was having trouble getting inspired, but then I saw Rodrick outside working on his van, and I got an idea.

Rory Screws Up
by Greg Heffley

Once upon a time there was this monkey named Rory.
The family he lived with loved him very much, even
though he was constantly screwing things up.

One day Rory accidentally rang the doorbell, and
everybody thought he did it on purpose. So they
gave him some bananas as a reward.

Well, now Rory was going around thinking he was some sort of monkey genius or something. And one day, he heard his owner say –

So Rory's primitive mind raced to formulate a plan. And here is what he eventually came up with:

Rory worked all day and all night, and to cut a long story short, the end result was not a fixed car.

After it was all over, Rory had learned a very valuable lesson: Rory is a monkey. And monkeys don't fix cars.

THE END

After I finished my paper, I showed it to Rodrick. I figured he wouldn't get it and, sure enough, I was right.

Like I said before, Rodrick knows he's got me under his thumb with this "secret" thing. So I have to get my kicks in any way I can.

<u>Wednesday</u>
Today was Manny's first day of pre-school, and apparently it didn't go so great.

All the other kids in Manny's school started back in September. But Manny wasn't potty trained until last week, so that's why he had to wait until now to make the jump from nursery.

Manny's pre-school was having their Halloween party today, so it wasn't the greatest way to introduce him to his classmates.

Manny's teachers had to call Mom at work and have her come get him.

I remember MY first day of pre-school. I didn't really know anyone, so I was pretty scared about being around a bunch of new kids. But this boy named Quinn came right over and started talking to me.

I didn't get that it was a joke, so it really freaked me out.

I told Mom I didn't want to go back to pre-school, and I told her all about Quinn and what he said.

But Mom told me Quinn was just being silly, and I didn't need to listen to him.

After Mom explained the joke, I actually thought it was pretty funny. I couldn't wait to go back to school the next day and try it out myself.

But it didn't really have the same effect.

NOVEMBER

<u>Monday</u>

It's been over a week since Rodrick's party, and I stopped worrying that Mom and Dad were gonna bust us for it. But remember that bathroom door we switched? Well, I forgot all about it until tonight.

Rodrick was upstairs in my room bugging me, and Dad went into the bathroom. A couple of seconds later, he said something that made Rodrick stop cold.

HEY...DIDN'T THIS DOOR USED TO LOCK?

I thought it was over. If Dad knew about the DOOR, it was just a matter of time before he found out about the party.

But Dad didn't put two and two together.

I MUST BE
LOSING MY
MARBLES.

AHHHHH...

You know, maybe it wouldn't be so bad if Mom
and Dad found out about the party. Rodrick
would get grounded, which would be AWESOME.
So if I can figure out a way to spill the beans
without Rodrick finding out, I'm gonna go for it.

Tuesday
I got my first letter from my French pen pal,
Mamadou, today. I decided to adjust my attitude
and give this whole pen-pal thing my best effort.
So when I wrote back to Mamadou today, I tried
to be as helpful as possible.

Dear Gregory,
    I am very privileged
to make your acquaintance.
                    Mamadou

Dear Mamadou,

I'm pretty sure "aquaintance"
doesn't have a "c" in it.

I really think you need to work
on your English.

                    Sincerely, Greg

I think it's dumb that Madame Lefrere won't let
us use e-mail with our pen pals. Albert Murphy
has already written back and forth with his pen
pal a bunch of times, and it's costing them a lot
of money in stamps.

Dear Jacques—	Dear Albert,	Dear Jacques—
How old are you?	12.	Oh.

COST: $14

<u>Friday</u>
Tonight, Rowley's parents went out to dinner,
so they got him a babysitter.

I don't know why Rowley can't just watch himself
for a few hours, but believe me I'm not complaining.
Rowley's babysitter is Heather Hills, and she's the
prettiest girl at Crossland High School.

So whenever the Jeffersons go out, I always make
sure to be up at Rowley's for "story time".

I went up to Rowley's at about 8:00 tonight. I
even splashed on some of Rodrick's cologne to make
sure I made a good impression on Heather.

I knocked on the door and waited for Heather to answer. But I was caught a little off guard when Rowley's next-door neighbour Leland answered instead.

I can't believe Rowley's parents switched babysitters from Heather to LELAND. They should've at least checked with me before doing something stupid like THAT.

Once I realized Heather wasn't there, I turned round to go back home. But Rowley asked me if I wanted to hang out and play Magick and Monsters with him and Leland.

The only reason I said "yes" was because I thought it was some kind of video game. But then I found out that you play it with pencils and paper and these special dice, and that you're supposed to use your "imagination" or whatever.

It actually turned out to be pretty fun, mostly because in Magick and Monsters you can do all sorts of stuff you could never do in real life.

I LIGHT ROWLEY'S EYEBROWS WITH A TORCH.

OUUUCHHH...

When I got home, I told Mom all about Magick and Monsters and how Leland was a really awesome Dungeon Keeper. Rodrick overheard me talking about Leland, and he said that Leland is the biggest nerd at his high school.

But this is coming from a guy who spends his Saturday nights putting fake throw-up on people's cars in the Home Depot parking lot. So I think I'll just take Rodrick's opinion with a grain of salt.

Wednesday

I've been going up to Leland's house every day after school to play Magick and Monsters. I was headed up there again today when Mom stopped me at the door.

Mom has been acting real suspicious of this whole Magick and Monsters thing.

And, from the questions she's been asking me, I guess she must think Leland is teaching me and Rowley witchcraft or something. So, today, Mom said she wanted to go WITH me to Leland's to watch us play.

I BEGGED Mom not to come, because first of all I knew she would never approve of all the violence in the game.

And, second of all, I knew that having her in the room would totally ruin the whole experience for everyone.

When I begged Mom not to join us, it made her even MORE suspicious. So now there was no changing her mind.

Rowley and Leland couldn't have cared less that Mom came with me. But I couldn't enjoy myself, because I felt like a total dork playing in front of her.

UH... MY WIZARD TALROC UTTERS THE SPELL OF TALRUNE.

I figured Mom would eventually get bored and just go home, but she stuck around. And, right when I thought she was finally gonna leave, Mom said that SHE wanted to join in the game.

So Leland started setting up a character for Mom, even though I was trying to signal to him that it was a big mistake.

When Leland created a character for Mom, Mom told Leland she wanted HER character to be MY character's mother in the game.

I did some quick thinking and told Mom that all the characters in Magick and Monsters are orphans, so she couldn't be my mother.

And Mom believed me. But then she asked Leland if she could NAME her character "Mom", and he said "yes."

I have to give Mom credit for figuring out that loophole, but it totally ruined the rest of the game for me.

Even though Mom wasn't technically my mother in the game, she sure ACTED like she was.

At this one point, our characters were hanging out in a tavern waiting for a spy to arrive, and my dwarf, Grimlon, ordered a pint of mead. Mead is sort of like beer in Magick and Monsters, and I guess Mom didn't approve of THAT.

The worst part of the game was when we got into a battle situation. See, the whole point of Magick and Monsters is that you're supposed to kill as many monsters as possible so you can get points and move up in levels.

But I don't really think Mom got that concept.

After about an hour of things going like this, I decided to quit. So I gathered up my stuff, and me and Mom headed home.

On the way back, Mom was really talking up Magick and Monsters, saying how it could help me with my "maths skills" and stuff like that. All I can say is, I hope she isn't planning on becoming a regular at these games. Because the first chance I get "Mom" is getting handed over to a pack of orcs.

Thursday
After school today, Mom took me to the bookstore and bought just about every Magick and Monsters book on the shelf. She must've dropped about $200, and she didn't even make me cash in a single Mom Buck.

I realized maybe I judged Mom a little too quickly, and maybe it wasn't such a bad thing having her in our group after all.

I was all set to take my new books up to Leland's, but that's when I found out there was a catch.

Mom actually bought all those books so me and RODRICK could play Magick and Monsters together. She said it was a good way for the two of us to work out our differences.

Mom told Rodrick she wanted him to be the Dungeon Keeper, just like Leland. Then she dumped the pile of books on Rodrick's bed and told him to start studying up.

It was bad enough playing in front of Mom at Leland's house, but I knew playing with Rodrick would be about ten times worse.

Mom was serious about me and Rodrick playing together, so I knew I was gonna have to go through with it. I spent about an hour up in my room making up characters with names Rodrick couldn't make fun of, like "Joe" and "Bob".

Once I was finished, I met Rodrick in the kitchen, and we started our game.

YOU AND YOUR GROUP OF NERDS FALL INTO A PIT AND IT'S FULL OF DYNAMITE AND YOU BLOW UP. THE END.

I guess I should be grateful that it was over with quickly. And I just hope Mom saved her receipts on those books.

Friday

The teachers have really been cracking down on kids copying from each other this year. Remember how I said I was glad I got put next to Alex Aruda in Pre-Algebra? Well, THAT hasn't done me any good.

Mrs Lee is my Pre-Algebra teacher, and I'm guessing she also had Rodrick when he was in middle school. Because that woman watches me like a HAWK.

Sometimes I think it would be really cool if I had a glass eye or something like that. First of all, I could use it to play all sorts of wacky tricks on my friends.

But the main thing I'd use it for is to help me get better grades.

On the first day of school, I'd aim my glass eye down like this:

GLASS EYE — REAL EYE

Then I'd go up to the teacher and say, "Listen, I just wanted to tell you I have a glass eye. So don't go thinking I'm looking at other people's papers."

OKEE DOKE. THANKS FOR LETTING ME KNOW.

Then, during a test, I'd aim my glass eye down at my OWN paper, and I'd look at some brainy kid's paper with my REAL eye.

I could copy away! And the teacher would be too dumb to notice.

THAT POOR GLASS-EYE KID.

Unfortunately, I DON'T have a glass eye. So if Mom asks me why I flunked my pop quiz in Pre-Algebra today, that's my excuse.

Sunday

Rodrick has been hitting Mom and Dad up for cash lately, so I guess the Mom Bucks programme isn't really working out for him. Mom has tried to make Rodrick do more chores to earn some money, but that hasn't been going too well.

IS THIS HOW YOU DO IT?

YOU NEED TO BE USING A CLEAN RAG, SON!

But, tonight, Mom figured out a way Rodrick could earn some cash. My school sent home a newsletter saying that Music Education has been cancelled because of budget cuts, so parents should get their kids private music lessons.

Mom told Rodrick he could give ME private drum lessons, and that she would PAY him for it.

I think Mom came up with the idea because lately Rodrick's been telling everyone he's a "professional drummer".

There's this local show called the "Community Follies" where all the neighbourhood parents do a bunch of comedy skits, and it's been running in our local theatre for about two weeks.

The other night, the regular drummer got sick, so Rodrick filled in, and he got paid five bucks.

I don't know if that really makes Rodrick a "professional drummer", but that didn't stop me from using it to score points with the girls at school.

When Mom told Rodrick he should start giving me drum lessons, he wasn't too hot on the idea. But then Mom said she'd pay him ten dollars a lesson, and that I could get a bunch of my friends to sign up, too.

So now I've gotta recruit some people for Rodrick's Drum Academy. And I can already tell this isn't gonna be a lot of fun.

Monday

I couldn't get any of my friends to sign up for Rodrick's drum school except Rowley, and I kind of had to trick HIM into doing it. Rowley is always saying he wants to learn how to play the drums, but he wants to play the kind they use in marching bands.

I told Rowley I knew for a FACT that Rodrick was going to cover all that stuff in week four, and that got Rowley pretty excited.

I was just glad I wasn't gonna have to take drum lessons all by myself.

Rowley came over after school, and we went down to the basement to start our first lesson. Rodrick started us off with some pretty basic drum drills.

There was only one practice pad and two drumsticks, so Rowley had to use a paper plate and some plastic utensils. But I guess that's what happens when you're the last person to sign up for a class.

After about fifteen minutes, Rodrick got a call from Ward, and that put an end to our first lesson.

Mom wasn't too happy to see me and Rowley upstairs so soon, and she sent us back down to the basement. She said not to come up until Rodrick had at least given us a practice assignment. So he did.

<u>Tuesday</u>
Me and Rowley had drum lessons with Rodrick
again today.

Well, Rodrick might be a good drummer, but he's
not a good teacher. Me and Rowley tried our best
to do the drills Rodrick taught us, but every time
we messed up, Rodrick would get frustrated.

Eventually, he got so fed up that he took our
drumsticks away. Rodrick sat down at his drum
set and told us to "watch and learn". Then he
started doing this really long drum solo that
didn't have anything to do with the drills he
was teaching us.

Rodrick didn't even look up from his drum set
when me and Rowley left and went upstairs.

I'm not complaining, though. Because the way I
see it, this way everyone wins.

Thursday
We've got a History paper due the day before
Thanksgiving, and I'd better start getting serious
about it.

The teachers are getting a lot stricter about the quality of work we turn in, and the way I usually do things isn't working so good any more.

Last week we had a paper due in Science, and Mrs Breckman said we had to choose an animal to write about. So I picked the moose. I know I should have gone to the library and done research, but I just decided to wing it.

The Amazing Moose
by Greg Heffley

Diet: The moose eats many, many things, but the list would be way too long to put in this paper. So I will save us all some time by just listing the things that the moose does NOT eat.

BUBBLE GUM   METAL   PIZZA

YOUR PIZZA, SIR.

NO, REALLY... I COULDN'T.

Even though there are moose habitats set up all over the place, the moose is almost extinct.

Everybody knows the moose evolved from birds, just like people did. But somewhere along the line people got arms, and the moose got stuck with those useless horns.

THE END

I actually thought I did a pretty good job. But I guess Mrs Breckman must be an expert on mooses or something, because she made me go to the library and start the paper over from scratch.

And my NEXT paper isn't gonna be any easier. I have to write a poem about the 1900s for Mr Huff's class, and I don't know the first thing about History OR poetry. So I guess I'd better start hitting the books.

Monday

I was up at Rowley's playing board games yesterday, and the craziest thing happened. When Rowley was in the bathroom, I noticed that there was some play money sticking out of the box of one of the other games.

I couldn't believe my eyes. Because the play money inside that game was the EXACT same kind of money Mom uses for Mom Bucks.

When I counted it up, there was something like $100,000 in cash in that box.

It only took me about two seconds to figure out what to do next.

When I got home, I ran upstairs and stuffed the money under my mattress. I tossed and turned all night trying to figure out what to do with my new Mom Bucks.

I realized Mom would probably have some way of knowing the difference between phony Mom Bucks and the real thing. So this morning, I decided to try a little experiment.

I asked Mom if I could cash in some Mom Bucks so I could buy stamps to write to my pen pal. I was really nervous when I handed Mom the money.

But she took it without even blinking.

I can't believe my luck! I figure I can make this $100,000 last all the way through high school, and maybe even further. I might not even have to get a real job later on.

The trick will be to not cash in too much at one time, or Mom will know something's up.

And I have to remember to earn a few Mom Bucks for real here and there so she doesn't get too suspicious.

I will say one thing for sure, though, and it's that I won't be using the money Mom gave me to buy stamps.

I got a picture from my pen pal, Mamadou, in the mail yesterday, and that pretty much killed any chance of me writing back to HIM.

<u>Tuesday</u>

My big History paper is due tomorrow, but they've been saying all week that it's gonna snow about a FOOT tonight.

So I haven't really been sweating it all that much.

At around 10:00, I peeked out the window to see how many inches of snow were on the ground so far. But I couldn't believe my eyes when I pulled back the curtain.

Man, I was counting on school being CANCELLED tomorrow. I turned on the news to see what had happened, but the weather guy was telling a TOTALLY different story than he was three hours ago.

That meant I had to get cracking on my History paper. The problem was, it was too late to go to the library, and we don't have any books in our house that are about the 1900s. So I knew I had to think of something quick.

Then I had a great idea.

Dad has bailed Rodrick out a MILLION times on his school papers. So I figured he could help me, too.

I told Dad about my situation, thinking he'd jump right in and help. But I guess Dad has learned his lesson in that department.

Rodrick must have overheard me talking to Dad, because he told me I should follow him downstairs.

You know how Rodrick had Mr Huff, my History teacher, in middle school? Well, it turns out Mr Huff gave Rodrick's class the EXACT same assignment when he was in my grade.

Rodrick dug around in his junk drawer and found his old paper. And then he told me he'd sell it to me for five bucks.

I told him there was no WAY I'd do that.

I'll admit, it was pretty tempting. Because, number one, since all of Rodrick's assignments have gone through Dad, I knew Rodrick got a good grade on his paper. And, number two, it was in one of those clear plastic binders that teachers go crazy for.

Plus, I had a huge stash of Mom Bucks under my mattress upstairs, and I knew I could pay Rodrick with that.

But I couldn't do it. I mean, I've copied from people's papers on quizzes and stuff before, but BUYING a paper from someone would be taking it to a whole other level.

So I decided I was gonna just have to suck it up and do the paper myself.

I started doing some research on the computer, but at about midnight the worst possible thing happened: the power went out.

BLINK

POP

That's when I knew I was in some serious trouble. I knew I'd flunk History if I didn't turn in a paper. So even though I didn't want to, I decided to take Rodrick up on his offer.

I scraped together $500 in Mom Bucks and went down to the basement. But Rodrick didn't let me off that easy.

Rodrick told me his new price was $20,000 in Mom Bucks. I told him I didn't have it, so he just rolled over and went back to sleep.

At that point, I was really desperate. So I went upstairs and grabbed a big handful of thousand dollar bills and brought them down to Rodrick's room. I gave him the money, and he turned over the paper. I felt really bad about what I did, but I just tried not to think about it and went to sleep.

<u>Wednesday</u>

On the bus ride to school, I took Rodrick's paper out of my bag. But I took one look at it and knew something was seriously wrong.

First of all, the poem wasn't typed out. It was in Rodrick's own handwriting.

That's when it hit me: Dad only started doing Rodrick's papers for him once he got to HIGH school. So that meant this paper was Rodrick's OWN work.

I started reading Rodrick's paper to see if I could still use it. But apparently Rodrick was even worse about doing his research than ME.

A Hundred Years Ago
by Rodrick Heffley

Sometimes I sit and wonder
About stuff I don't know
Like what the heck the earth was like
A hundred years ago.

Did cavemen ride on dinosaurs?
Did flowers even grow?
Well we could guess but that was back
A hundred years ago.

I wish they built a time machine
And they picked me to go
To check out what the scene was like
A hundred years ago.

Did giant spiders rule the earth?
Were deserts filled with snow?
I wonder what the story was
A hundred years ago.

(F) See me!

I guess I learned my lesson about buying a paper from someone. Or at least from RODRICK.

When third period rolled around, I didn't have anything to turn in to Mr Huff. I guess that means I'll be taking summer school for History.

And my day got a whole lot worse after that. When I got home from school, Mom was waiting for me at the front door.

You know that stack of bills I paid Rodrick with? Well, he tried to cash them ALL in at once to get money for a used motorcycle. I'm sure Mom knew something was fishy, since Rodrick has never earned a single Mom Buck on his own.

Rodrick told Mom where he got the money, and she dug around my room until she found my stash under the mattress. Mom knew she never put $100,000 into circulation, so she confiscated ALL my cash, even the ones I earned for real. I guess that's the end of the Mom Bucks programme.

To be honest with you, I'm kind of relieved. Sleeping on that pile of cash every night was really stressing me out.

Mom was mad that I tried to put one over on her like that, so she gave me a punishment. But I got that out of the way before dinner.

MOM SAYS WE HAVE TO CLEAN THE WHOLE GARAGE.

SHOOT.

Today was Thanksgiving, and it started off like
it always does: with Aunt Loretta showing up
two hours early.

Mom always makes me and Rodrick "entertain"
Aunt Loretta, and that means talk to her until
the rest of the family shows up.

The biggest fights me and Rodrick have ever had
were over who has to greet her first.

The rest of the family started trickling in at around 11:00. Dad's brother, Uncle Joe, and his kids were the last ones to show up at around 12:30.

Uncle Joe's kids all call Dad the same thing.

HI, AUNT FWANK!

Mom thinks it's really cute, but Dad swears that Uncle Joe tells his kids to do it on purpose.

Things are pretty tense between Dad and Uncle Joe, because Dad is still mad at Uncle Joe for something he did LAST Thanksgiving. Back then, Manny had just started potty training, and he was doing pretty good. In fact, he was probably about two weeks from being out of diapers.

But Uncle Joe said something to Manny that changed everything.

It was six months before Manny would even step foot in the bathroom again.

Every time Dad changed a dirty diaper after that, I heard him cursing Uncle Joe under his breath.

We had dinner around 2:00, and then people went into the living room to talk. I didn't feel like talking, so I went in the family room to play video games.

Eventually, I guess Dad had enough of the family, too, so he went downstairs to work on his Civil War battlefield. But he forgot to lock the door to the furnace room, and Uncle Joe walked in after him.

Uncle Joe seemed pretty interested in what Dad was working on, so Dad told him all about it.

Dad gave Uncle Joe this big speech about the 150th Regiment and the role it played at Gettysburg, and spent about a half hour describing the whole battle.

But I don't think Uncle Joe was really listening to Dad's speech.

NICE TOYS, BIG BROTHER!

Thanksgiving didn't last too much longer after that. Dad went upstairs and turned up the thermostat until it got stuffy and everyone cleared out. And that's pretty much how Thanksgiving ends every year at our house.

DECEMBER

Saturday

You remember how I said Mom and Dad were going to eventually find out about Rodrick's party? Well, it finally happened today.

Mom sent Dad out to pick up the pictures from Thanksgiving, and when Dad got back, you could tell he wasn't happy about something.

The picture in Dad's hand was from Rodrick's party.

It looked like one of Rodrick's friends accidentally took a picture with Mom's camera, which she keeps on the shelf above the stereo. And when he took the picture, it captured the whole scene.

Rodrick tried to deny that he had a party. But everything was right there in the picture, so there really wasn't any point.

Mom and Dad took away Rodrick's car keys and told him his punishment is that he's not allowed to leave the house for a whole MONTH.

They were even mad at ME, because they said I was Rodrick's "accomplice". So I got hit with a two-week video-game ban.

Sunday
Mom and Dad have been all over Rodrick's case ever since they found out about his party. Rodrick usually sleeps until 2:00 in the afternoon on weekends, but today Dad made Rodrick get out of bed by 8:00 a.m.

Making Rodrick get out of bed early is a pretty big blow to him, because Rodrick LOVES to sleep. One time last fall, Rodrick slept for thirty-six hours STRAIGHT.

He slept all the way from Sunday night until Tuesday morning, and he didn't even realize he missed a whole day of his life until Tuesday night.

But it looks like Rodrick has found a way around the new 8:00 rule. Now, when Dad tells Rodrick to get out of bed, Rodrick just drags his stuff upstairs with him and he sleeps on the couch until it's time for dinner. So I guess you gotta give this round to Rodrick.

<u>Tuesday</u>
Mom and Dad are going away again this weekend,
and they're dropping me and Rodrick off at
Grandpa's. They said they WERE gonna let us
stay home, but we proved we can't be trusted on
our own.

Grandpa lives over in Leisure Towers, which is
this old folks' home. I had to spend a week
there with Rodrick a few months ago, and it was
the low point of my whole summer.

Manny is staying with Gramma this weekend, and
I'd give ANYTHING to trade places with him.
Gramma always has her fridge stocked with soda
and cake and stuff like that, and she has cable
TV with all the movie channels.

The reason Manny is going to Gramma's is because Manny is Gramma's favourite. And all you need to do is take one look at her refrigerator for the proof.

But, if anyone ever accuses Gramma of showing favourites, she gets all defensive.

And it's not just the pictures on the fridge, either. Gramma has Manny's drawings and stuff hanging up all over the house.

The only thing that Gramma has from ME is this note I wrote her when I was six. I was mad at her because she wouldn't give me any ice cream before dinner, so here's what I wrote:

I hate you Gram-ma

Gramma has kept that note all these years, and she's STILL holding it over my head.

AND THIS IS WHAT MY WONDERFUL GRANDSON GREGORY MADE FOR ME!

I guess every grandparent has their favourite, and I can understand that. But at least Grandpa is up front about it.

GREGORY IS MY FAVOURITE!

Saturday

Well, Mom and Dad dumped me and Rodrick off at Grandpa's today, just like they said they were gonna do.

I started looking for ways to entertain myself, but there's nothing in Grandpa's condo that's fun to do, so I just sat down with him and watched TV. But Grandpa doesn't even watch real shows. He just keeps his TV tuned to the security camera that's in the front lobby of his building.

And after a few hours of THAT, you start to go a little nuts.

At about 5:00, Grandpa made us dinner. Grandpa makes this awful thing called "watercress salad", and it's the worst thing you ever tasted.

It's basically a bunch of cold green beans and cucumbers floating in a pool of vinegar.

Rodrick knows I hate watercress salad more than ANYTHING, so the last time we stayed at Grandpa's, Rodrick made sure to pile it on my plate.

I had to sit there and choke down every bite so Grandpa's feelings wouldn't be hurt.

And guess what I got as a reward for cleaning my plate?

Tonight, Grandpa gave us our salad, and I acted like I was gonna eat it. But then I just stuffed it all in my pocket when no one was looking.

It felt pretty disgusting when the cold vinegar started running down my leg, but believe me it was about a thousand times better than having to EAT it.

DRIP

After dinner, the three of us went into the living room. Grandpa has all these really old board games, and he always makes me and Rodrick play them with him.

He has this one game called "Gutbusters", where one player reads a card, and the other player tries not to laugh.

I always beat Grandpa, mostly because the jokes don't make any sense to me.

I always beat Rodrick, too, but that's because Rodrick loses on purpose. Whenever it's my turn to read a card, he makes sure he has a big mouthful of milk.

At 10:00, I was ready for bed. But Rodrick bagged the couch, and that meant I had to sleep with Grandpa again.

All I can say is, if Mom and Dad were trying to teach me a lesson for covering for Rodrick, well, mission accomplished.

COULD YOU PUT MY TEETH IN THAT GLASS?

Sunday

Rodrick has a big Science Fair project due right before Christmas break, and it looks like Mom and Dad are making Rodrick do this one all by himself.

Last year, Rodrick's science project was called
"Does Watching Violent Movies Make People Think
Violent Thoughts?".

I guess the idea was to have people watch horror
movies and then draw pictures afterwards to show
how the movies affected them.

But it was really just an excuse for Rodrick and
his friends to watch a bunch of horror movies on
school nights.

Rodrick's friends got the movie-watching part
done, but they didn't draw a single picture. And
the night before the Science Fair, Rodrick didn't
have anything to show for himself.

169

So me, Mom and Dad had to bail Rodrick out. Dad typed up the paper, Mom made the poster board stuff and I had to draw a bunch of pictures.

I did my best to imagine what teenagers would draw after watching violent movies.

The thing that REALLY stinks is that I caught heat from Mom when she saw my drawings, because she said they were "disturbing". And that's why I was only allowed to watch G-rated movies for the rest of the year.

But if you want to talk about "disturbing", you should've seen some of the stuff Manny was coming up with those days.

One night, Rodrick accidentally left one of his
horror movies in the DVD player and, when
Manny went to turn on cartoons the next day,
he got Rodrick's movie instead.

I came across a couple of Manny's drawings
after that, and some of them were enough to
give ME nightmares.

<u>Tuesday</u>

Mom and Dad set up due dates for Rodrick on his Science Fair project, and by 6:00 tonight, he was supposed to tell them the theme of his experiment.

But at 6:45, things weren't looking so good.

Rodrick was watching a show about astronauts, and what happens to them after they've been up in space for a long time. The show said that when the astronauts get back to Earth, they're actually TALLER than when they left.

And the reason is because there's no gravity in space, so their spines decompress or something.

Well, that gave Rodrick the idea he was looking for.

Rodrick told Mom and Dad he was going to do his science experiment on the effect of "zero gravity" on the human spine. And, from the way Rodrick was talking it up, you'd think the results of his experiment were gonna benefit mankind.

Dad seemed pretty impressed. Or maybe he was just relieved that Rodrick actually came through on his first task. But I think Dad started to see things a little differently later on when he told Rodrick to take the trash out to the kerb.

<u>Wednesday</u>
Yesterday at school, they announced tryouts for the big Winter Talent Show.

As soon as I found out about it, I came up with this AWESOME idea for a comedy skit that me and Rowley could do. But I admit the REAL reason I wrote it was to give myself an excuse to talk to Holly Hills, who is Heather Hills's sister and the most popular girl in my grade.

CREDITS

WRITER - GREG HEFFLEY
DIRECTOR - GREG HEFFLEY
DAD - GREG HEFFLEY
MOM - HOLLY HILLS
DOG-BOY - ROWLEY JEFFERSON

I showed Rowley the script, but he wasn't too enthusiastic about the idea.

SHOVE

You'd think Rowley would be grateful that I was gonna make him a big star. But, like Mom always says, there are some people you just can't please.

Thursday
Rowley went and found someone ELSE to partner
with for the Talent Show. He's gonna do a magic
act with this kid from his karate class named
Scotty Douglas.

And, if you want to know if I'm jealous, let me
put it to you this way: Scotty Douglas is in the
FIRST GRADE. So Rowley will be lucky if he
doesn't get beaten up at school for this.

They're having one big Talent Show for the
elementary school, the middle school and the high
school. So that means Rodrick and his band are
gonna be in the same competition as Rowley and
Scotty Douglas.

Rodrick's ALL fired up about the Talent Show.
His band has never played in front of a crowd,
so they see this as their big chance to get noticed.

Rodrick is still grounded, but the rule is that he's not allowed to leave the house. So his band just comes over every day and practises down in the basement. I think Dad's starting to wish he had worded Rodrick's punishment a little differently.

But if Rodrick's band really thinks they can win this Talent Show, they'd better get serious and play some actual music. Because they spent their last two practices fooling around with a new echo pedal they got over the weekend.

Friday

Dad ended Rodrick's punishment two weeks early, because he was going bonkers listening to Löded Diper practise every day. So, tonight, Rodrick went to his friend Ward's for the weekend.

With Rodrick out of the house, that meant the basement was free. So I invited Rowley over to spend the night.

Me and Rowley bought a bunch of candy and soda, and Rowley brought over his portable TV. We even managed to get our hands on a couple of Rodrick's horror movies, so we were all set. But then Mom came downstairs with Manny.

LOOK WHO CAME TO **JOIN** YOU!

The only reason Mom dumped Manny on us was so he could spy and tell her if we were doing anything wrong.

Every single time I've had a sleepover, Manny has ruined it. The last time Rowley slept over was the WORST.

Manny must've got cold in the middle of the night, so he crawled into Rowley's sleeping bag to get warm.

That freaked Rowley out enough to make him go home early. And he hasn't been back to spend the night ever since.

It looked like Manny was gonna ruin ANOTHER sleepover. Me and Rowley couldn't watch our horror movies with Manny around, so we decided to just play board games instead.

But I'm a little sick of board games and, besides, Rowley was kind of driving me crazy.

He needed to go to the bathroom every five minutes, and whenever he'd come back downstairs, he'd kick a pillow across the room.

BOOH-YAH!

KICK

It might have been funny the first couple of times, but then it really started getting on my nerves. So the next time Rowley went upstairs to use the bathroom, I played a prank on him.

I put one of Dad's dumbbells underneath a pillow. And sure enough, the next time Rowley came downstairs, he gave it a big kick.

Well, that did it. Rowley started blubbering like a baby, and I couldn't quiet him down.

And with all the racket Rowley was making, Mom came downstairs.

Mom took a look at Rowley's big toe, and she seemed pretty concerned. I think Mom's sensitive about Rowley getting injured in our house after the tinfoil-ball incident, so she drove him right home.

I was just glad she didn't ask us how it happened.

As soon as Mom and Rowley walked out of the door, I knew I'd better start working on Manny.

Manny saw me put that dumbbell under the pillow, and I knew he would tell Mom what I did. So I came up with an idea to keep him from snitching.

I packed some bags and told Manny I was gonna run away from home so I didn't have to face Mom for what I did.

Then I walked out the door and acted like I was leaving for good.

GOODBYE, O FAMILY. GOODBYE, GOODBYE, GOODBYE!

I got that idea from Rodrick. He used to pull the same kind of thing on me when HE did something bad and he knew I was gonna tell on HIM. He would act like he was running away, and then, five minutes later, he would just walk back inside.

And by that time, I was ready to forgive him for whatever he did.

So after I told Manny I was leaving home, I shut the door and waited outside for a few minutes. And when I opened the door, I expected to find him crying in the foyer. But Manny wasn't where I left him. I started walking around the house looking for him, and guess where he was?

Down in the basement, eating my candy.

Anyway, if letting Manny eat my candy is the price I have to pay to keep him quiet, I can live with it.

Saturday
After I woke up this morning, I went down to the kitchen. But one look at Mom's face told me that Manny sold me out.

Manny told Mom everything. He even told her about our horror movies. Don't even ask me how he knew about THAT.

Mom made me call Rowley to apologize, but then she made me talk to his parents and apologize to THEM, too. So I don't think I'm going to get invited back over to Rowley's house any time soon.

Then Mom got on the phone with Mrs Jefferson. Mrs Jefferson said Rowley's big toe was broken, and that he had to stay off it for a week.

Then Mrs. Jefferson said Rowley is "heartbroken", because this means he'll have to miss the Talent Show tryouts. And he's been practising his magic act with Scotty Douglas all week.

So Mom told Mrs Jefferson that I would be HAPPY to fill in for Rowley at the tryouts. I started tugging at Mom's sleeve to let her know this was a TERRIBLE idea, but of course she just ignored me.

After Mom got off the phone, I told her the last thing I needed at school is to be onstage doing magic tricks with a kid who was in pull-ups a year ago.

But Mom made me go through with it anyway. She took me down to Scotty's house and explained the situation to his mother. So now there was no getting out of it.

Mrs Douglas invited me inside, and me and
Scotty went up to his room to start practising.
Well, the first thing I found out was that
Rowley and Scotty were not equal partners in this
act. Rowley was actually Scotty's ASSISTANT.

I told Scotty there was no WAY I was gonna
be a magician's assistant to a first-grader. But
Scotty said it was HIS magic set, and he started
throwing a big tantrum.

So I just went along with the idea to keep
Scotty quiet, because, believe me, I did not need
any more trouble.

Then Scotty handed me this shirt that was covered
with all these sparkly sequins, and he told me
that it was my costume.

It looked like something Gramma would wear to Bingo. I told Scotty maybe I could wear something cooler, like a leather jacket, but he said that wouldn't be "magic" enough.

Anyway, it turns out all I have to do for the act is hand Scotty a prop every once in a while, so maybe it really isn't going to be all that bad.

But ask me how I feel again if we get in and have to perform onstage in front of five hundred people instead of Scotty's baby sister.

Sunday
I'll tell you ONE good thing that's come out of practising this magic act with Scotty Douglas: it's given me a bunch of good ideas for more Creighton the Cretin comics.

Rowley quit doing his comic strip "Zoo-Wee Mama!" for the school paper a few months ago, because he said he wanted to have more time to play with his Dinoblazer action figures. That means the cartoonist job is open again, and maybe I have a shot.

I'M GONNA MAKE THIS APPLE DISAPPEAR.

OH, BOY!

TA DA!

YOU DIDN'T MAKE IT DISAPPEAR, YOU JUST ATE IT!

UH OH, YOU FIGURED OUT MY TRICK.

YOU DIDN'T EVEN EAT THE WHOLE THING!

OK, WATCH THIS. NOW AIN'T **THAT** MAGIC?

THAT'S NOT MAGIC, IT'S JUST A LIGHTER!

FLICK

OOPS. I THOUGHT IT WAS MAGIC.

BOO! YOU'RE NOT A MAGICIAN, YOU'RE AN IDIOT!

PLUS, THAT'S NOT EVEN A MAGICIAN'S HAT. IT'S AN ABRAHAM LINCOLN HAT!

OOPS.

THE END.

<u>Monday</u>
Well, good news on the Talent Show. The tryouts were today, and me and Scotty didn't make it in.

OK, so maybe I could have done a better job as Scotty's assistant. But I didn't blow it on PURPOSE. I just forgot to hand him his props once or twice.

We were the ONLY ones who didn't make the cut, and that actually is kind of embarrassing.

I know we weren't exactly the best act trying out today, but we weren't the WORST, either. Some of the acts that got in were a lot lamer than our magic act.

This kindergartner named Harry Gilbertson made the cut, and all he did was roller-skate figure eights around a boom box that was playing "Yankee Doodle Dandy".

Rodrick's band made it in, too, and he's acting like that's some huge accomplishment.

Like I said before, Rodrick is really excited about the Winter Talent Show. In fact, he actually got his Science Fair project done a day EARLY so he could squeeze in some extra band practices before the big night.

But when Rodrick turned in his project, his Science teacher told him he was gonna have to start over and come up with a whole new idea. He said that Rodrick didn't use the "scientific method" with a hypothesis and a conclusion and all that.

Rodrick told the teacher he actually grew a sixteenth of an inch during his "zero gravity" experiment, so that proved he was on to something.

But his teacher said that's a normal amount for a boy Rodrick's age to grow in a month.

Well, this really stinks for me, because I had decided to do my Science Fair project on "zero gravity", too.

And now it looks like all the research I did was just a big waste of time.

Dad told Rodrick he's going to have to just skip the Talent Show so he can do a new experiment, but Rodrick says he's not going to do it.

Rodrick told Dad he doesn't CARE about school any more. He said his plan is to win the talent show and use the tape of the performance to get signed to a record label. Then he'll quit school and just do the band full-time.

It sounds like a terrible plan to me, but I think Dad is pretty open to the idea.

<u>Wednesday</u>

Tonight was the big Winter Talent Show. I didn't want to go, and neither did Dad. But Mom made us both go to show our support for Rodrick.

Rodrick and Mom went to the school early to bring some stuff that Rodrick's band needed, so Dad had to ride in the band's van with Bill. And Dad wasn't too thrilled when he ran into his boss in the school parking lot.

The show kicked off at 7:00 and, let me just say, I think it was a really bad idea to combine the three schools for this thing.

195

They ended up having kindergartners singing songs to their teddy bears followed by eighteen-year-olds doing speed metal guitar solos.

I don't think Dad approved of Larry Larkin and all his piercings. Halfway through Larry's guitar solo, Dad leaned over and whispered to the man sitting next to him.

I wish I had time to warn Dad that the guy he was talking to was Larry's father.

"HI, DAD!"

Another problem with combining the schools was that there were too many acts, and the show went on FOREVER.

At 9:30 they decided to start running two acts at the same time to keep the show moving along. Sometimes it worked out all right, like when they had Patty Farrell tap-dancing while Spencer Kitt was juggling. But other times it didn't work out too good, like when Terrence James played a harmonica on a unicycle while Charise Kline read her poem about global warming.

Rodrick's band was the last act to take the stage.

Before the show, Rodrick asked me to videotape his band during their act, but I told him no WAY.

He's been such a jerk to me lately that I can't believe he was trying to get me to do him a favour. So Mom volunteered for camera duty.

Rodrick's band got paired up with Harry Gilbertson, the roller-skating kid. And I'm sure Rodrick wasn't too happy about THAT.

I noticed Dad wasn't sitting next to me while Rodrick's band played, so I looked around for him.

Dad was standing in the back of the gym with cotton balls sticking out of his ears, and he stayed there until the song was over.

After Rodrick's band performed, they handed out the awards. Rodrick's band didn't win anything, but Harry Gilbertson walked away with the prize for "Best Musical Act".

But you'll never guess who the Grand Prize Winner was: Rowley's babysitter, Leland.

He won for his ventriloquist act, because the judges said it was "wholesome".

I never thought I'd agree with Rodrick on anything, but I'm starting to wonder if maybe he was right about Leland being a nerd after all.

HEY, WHO'S THE DUMMY HERE?

After the show, Rodrick's band came back to our house to watch the videotape of their performance.

They were all grumbling about how they got "robbed", and how the judges don't know the first thing about rock and roll.

So their plan was to just mail the videotape off to some record labels and let their performance speak for itself.

They all sat down in front of the TV and Rodrick put the tape in the machine. But it took about thirty seconds for everyone to realize the tape was worthless.

You know how Rodrick asked Mom to videotape the show? Well, she did a pretty good job of filming, but she talked nonstop during the first two minutes. And the camera picked up every little comment she made.

THAT SHIRT MAKES RODRICK'S ARMS LOOK SO SKINNY!

Every time Bill stuck out his tongue and flicked it up and down like a rock star, you could hear Mom ring in with her opinion.

I DON'T LIKE THAT!

In fact, the only time Mom stopped talking was when Rodrick did his drum solo. But during that part the camera was shaking around so much that you couldn't even see anything.

At first, Rodrick and his bandmates were really mad. But then one of them remembered that the school taped the Talent Show, and it's supposed to be on the local cable channel tomorrow night.

I guess that means they'll all be coming back over to watch THAT.

Thursday

Well, things have got REALLY bad for me in the last few hours.

Rodrick and his bandmates came over at around 7:00 tonight to watch the Talent Show on TV. They sat through the whole three-hour show until their band came on.

The school actually did a decent job of taping the performance, and things were looking pretty good up until Rodrick's drum solo.

That's when Mom started dancing. And whoever was doing the filming zoomed right in on Mom, and kept the camera pointed at her for the rest of the song.

That meant Rodrick didn't have ANYTHING he could send to record companies. And he was really mad about it, too.

At first he was mad at Mom for messing things up. But Mom said that if Rodrick didn't want people to dance, he shouldn't play music.

Then Rodrick turned on ME. He said this was all MY fault, because if I just taped the show like he asked me to, none of this would've happened.

But I told him that maybe if he wasn't such a jerk, I would have done it for him.

We started to yell at each other. Mom and Dad broke us up, and then they sent Rodrick down to his room and me up to mine.

But a couple of hours later I went downstairs, and I ran into Rodrick in the kitchen. He was smiling, so I knew something was up.

Rodrick told me my "secret was out".

At first, I didn't know what he was talking about. But then I got it: he was talking about the thing that happened to me this summer.

I ran down to the basement, and I picked up Rodrick's phone to see if he had made any calls. And, sure enough, it looked like he had called EVERY friend of his who had a brother or sister my age.

By tomorrow morning, EVERYONE at my school will know the story. And I'm sure Rodrick exaggerated the facts to make the story sound even WORSE.

Now that my secret's out there, I want to put on record what REALLY happened, and not Rodrick's twisted version.

So here it goes.

Over the summer, me and Rodrick had to stay with Grandpa at his condo in Leisure Towers for a few days. But there was NOTHING to do, and I was going bonkers.

I was so bored, I broke out my old journal and started to write in it. But taking out a book that said "diary" on the cover in front of Rodrick was a HUGE mistake.

Rodrick stole my journal and made a run for it. He probably would have made it into the bathroom and locked the door if someone hadn't left Gutbusters sitting out.

I scooped the book off the floor and ran out into the hallway and down the stairwell. Then I ducked into the bathroom in the main lobby and locked myself in a stall.

I kept my feet off the floor so that if Rodrick came in, he wouldn't know I was in there.

I knew that if Rodrick got hold of my journal, it would be a nightmare. So I decided to just rip the whole thing into tiny little pieces and flush them down the toilet. It was better to just destroy the thing than risk Rodrick getting his hands on it.

But as soon as I started ripping pages out of the book, I heard the bathroom door open. I thought it was Rodrick, so I just stayed completely still.

I didn't hear anything, so I peeked over the top of the stall to see what was going on. That's when I saw a woman standing in front of the mirror, putting on make-up.

I figured the lady just accidentally wandered into the men's room, because people at Leisure Towers are always doing stuff like that.

I was about to speak up and tell this lady she was in the wrong bathroom, but right then someone else walked in. And guess what? It was ANOTHER woman.

That's when I realized that I was the one who messed up, and I was in the WOMEN's bathroom.

I prayed that those ladies would just wash their hands and leave so I could make a run for it. But they sat down in the stalls on either side of me. And every time one woman would leave the bathroom, someone else would come in and take their place. So I couldn't leave.

If Rowley thinks he had it bad when those kids made him eat the Cheese, he should try being stuck in the Leisure Towers ladies' room for an hour and a half.

I guess someone eventually heard me in there, and they reported me to the front desk. Within a few minutes, word got around the building that there was a "Peeping Tom" in the women's room.

By the time security came in and got me out of there, everyone who lived in Leisure Towers was down in the lobby. And Rodrick saw the whole thing unfold upstairs on Grandpa's TV.

Now that the story was out, I knew I couldn't show my face at school. So I told Mom she was gonna have to transfer me somewhere else, and I told her why.

Mom said I shouldn't worry about what other people think. She told me that my classmates would understand that I had just made an "honest mistake".

So that just proves once and for all that Mom doesn't understand a THING about kids my age.

Now I'm kicking myself for not keeping up my pen-pal relationship with Mamadou. Because if me and him had stayed in touch, maybe I could have gone to France as an exchange student and hid out THERE for a few years.

All I know is, the one place I don't want to go tomorrow is school. And it looks like that's exactly where I'm headed.

Friday
The CRAZIEST thing happened today. When I walked in the door at school, a bunch of guys cornered me, and I braced myself for the teasing to start. But instead of harassing me they started CONGRATULATING me.

Everyone was shaking my hand and patting me on the back, and I didn't know WHAT was going on.

With all those guys talking to me at the same time, it took me a while to make sense of anything. But here's what must have happened.

The story Rodrick told his friends got passed on to their brothers and sisters, and then they told THEIR friends.

But by the time word spread around, all the details got totally messed up.

So the story went from me accidentally walking into the women's bathroom at Leisure Towers to me infiltrating the girls' locker room at Crossland HIGH SCHOOL.

I couldn't believe everything got twisted like that, but I wasn't about to set the record straight, either.

All of a sudden, I was the hero at school. I even got a nickname. People were calling me the "Stealthinator".

Someone even made me a Stealthinator headband, and you better believe I wore it. Things like this NEVER happen to me, so I wasn't gonna pass up my moment of glory.

And for the first time ever I knew what it felt like to be the most popular kid at school.

Unfortunately, the girls weren't as impressed with me as the guys were. In fact, I think I might have a little trouble getting someone to go to the Valentine's Dance with me.

Monday

You know how Rodrick wanted his band to get noticed? Well, he kind of got his wish, because EVERYBODY knows who Löded Diper is now.

I guess somebody must have thought the tape of Mom cutting loose at the Talent Show was pretty funny, because it's all over the Internet. And now everyone knows Rodrick Heffley as the drummer from the "Dancing Mom" video.

Ever since, Rodrick's been hiding out in the basement, waiting for the whole thing to blow over. And I have to admit I do feel kind of sorry for him.

I'm getting teased about the video at school too, but at least I'm not IN it.

And, even though Rodrick can be a huge jerk sometimes, he IS my brother.

Tomorrow is the Science Fair, and if Rodrick doesn't turn in a project, he's gonna flunk out of school.

So that's why I offered to help him out with his project, but just this one last time. We worked together all night, and I don't mean to brag, but we did a really good job.

Anyway, when Rodrick gets First Prize tomorrow and passes Science, I just hope he realizes how lucky he is to have a brother like ME.

ACKNOWLEDGEMENTS

I'll be forever grateful to my family for providing the inspiration, encouragement and support I need to create these books. A huge thanks goes to my brothers, Scott and Pat; my sister, Re; and to my mom and dad. Without you, there would be no Heffleys. Thanks to my wife, Julie, and my kids, who have made so many sacrifices to make my dream of being a cartoonist come true. Thanks also to my in-laws, Tom and Gail, who have been there with a helping hand during every deadline.

Thanks to the terrific folks at Abrams, especially Charlie Kochman, an incredibly dedicated editor and a remarkable human being, and to those people at Abrams with whom I've had the pleasure of working most closely: Jason Wells, Howard Reeves, Susan Van Metre, Chad Beckerman, Samara Klein, Valerie Ralph and Scott Auerbach. A special thanks goes to Michael Jacobs.

Thanks to Jess Brallier for bringing Greg Heffley to the world on Funbrain.com. Thanks to Betsy Bird (Fuse #8) for wielding her considerable influence to spread the word about *Diary of a Wimpy Kid*. Lastly, thanks to Dee Sockol-Frye, and to all of the booksellers across the country who put these books into kids' hands.

ABOUT THE AUTHOR

Jeff Kinney is a #1 *New York Times* bestselling author and a five-time Nickelodeon Kids' Choice Award winner for Favourite Book. Jeff has been named one of *Time* magazine's 100 Most Influential People in the World. He is also the creator of Poptropica, which was named one of *Time* magazine's 50 Best Websites. He spent his childhood in the Washington, D.C., area and moved to New England in 1995. Jeff lives with his wife and two sons in Massachusetts, where they own a bookstore, An Unlikely Story.